Trapped in Battle Royale
Book Two

BATTLE FOR LOOT LAKE

AN UNOFFICIAL NOVEL OF FORTNITE

Devin Hunter

Sky Pony Press
New York

Copyright © 2018 by Hollan Publishing, Inc.

Fortnite® is a registered trademark of Epic Games, Inc.

The Fortnite game is copyright © Epic Games, Inc.

Sky Pony Press books may be purchased in bulk at special discounts for sales promotion, corporate gifts, fund-raising, or educational purposes. Special editions can also be created to specifications. For details, contact the Special Sales Department, Sky Pony Press, 307 West 36th Street, 11th Floor, New York, NY 10018 or info@skyhorsepublishing.com.

Sky Pony® is a registered trademark of Skyhorse Publishing, Inc.®, a Delaware corporation.

Visit our website at www.skyponypress.com.

10 9 8 7 6 5 4 3 2

Library of Congress Cataloging-in-Publication Data is available on file.

Cover design by Brian Peterson
Cover artwork by Amanda Brack

Paperback ISBN: 978-1-5107-4264-2
E-book ISBN: 978-1-5107-4267-3

Printed in Canada

CHAPTER ONE

Grey hated when his squad picked Tomato Town as a starting place. Not because it was a bad spot, or because there was always a chance they'd die early when lots of others showed up. It was because of the pizza place. It made him miss home. And pizza. Food in general, really.

It had been three weeks since Grey had gotten sucked into this virtual reality version of Fortnite Battle Royale, and he was homesick. More than he had ever been.

He hadn't told anyone, since it didn't seem fair to complain when two of his squad mates, Ben and Tristan, had been stuck in this world for almost a year. But as Grey's squad fortified their

1

position in the pizza place, he wished he could feel his stomach rumble. He wanted to feel hungry so he'd have to eat. It was strange, not having a real body to do those things. His mind still wanted to do them. More than missing his body, he missed his family and friends. He missed his room and even his school. He missed being a *person*.

It felt more and more that he was just a character in a video game.

Grey took a shot to his shoulder, and his shield was almost gone.

"Focus, Grey!" Kiri yelled at him.

"Sorry!" He tried to shake off the homesickness. "This place always makes me miss pizza!"

Ben groaned. "What I'd do for a piece of pizza . . . extra cheese, pepperoni, and olives."

"Not you, too!" Tristan said as he laid a trap on the wall.

"How can you not miss pizza?" Ben asked.

Tristan shrugged. "I miss my mother's schnitzel. Pizza is so . . . American. I do miss German food, though."

"Pizza is international," Kiri said. "We love it in New Zealand. You're just weird."

Grey laughed.

"I could do with a fresh slice of my Auntie Ripeka's Maori bread, though," Kiri said with a sigh.

"I don't know what that is, but if it's bread, I'll like it," Ben said.

They were probably doomed to be eliminated very soon, being holed up here, but at least his squad was getting along.

And they had been getting better.

Depending on the day, Grey's squad averaged being ranked in the fifties and forties. For a moment one day, they were even in the thirties. Even now, there were already sixty people eliminated.

Once the wall was broken down, the first enemy to run in died on the trap. Grey unloaded with his weapon, but the second he heard the C4, he knew this would be the end of the current battle. Sure enough, they all took critical damage, but at least they were laughing as their vision went black and white.

Having fun took the edge off missing home.

"Coulda been worse," Ben said. "We did decent for the day."

"Yeah, just positioning bad luck," Tristan replied. It was strange to think that, three weeks ago, Tristan had left their squad and fought with Ben. Now it seemed like it had never happened.

"The storm is not our mate," Kiri said.

"Maybe tomorrow." Grey had played enough battles to know that sometimes luck wasn't on your side. Sometimes you got bad weapons. Sometimes the eye of the storm ended up on the opposite side of the map. All one hundred players stuck there had had some bad days at this point, and the average rankings had only gotten tighter together.

As they waited for the battle to be over, Grey selected a player who was still alive to watch. His favorite had become Tae Min, the top player in the whole group.

Grey figured a lot of people watched Tae Min, but it was hard not to. There was so much to learn from spectating. Tae Min wasn't just a good shooter—he could also build at lightning speed. He didn't just know every location—he knew how to use them to his advantage. And on top of all that, it felt like Tae Min was a mind reader.

Sure enough, Tae Min was one of the very last ones alive. His ranking had only fallen to five from his perfect first day. The next closest player, a teen girl named Hui Yin, had a ranking of twelve.

Tae Min was in the eye of the storm building a tower faster than Grey could imagine doing. It made Grey want to practice more.

A squad of players tried to get Tae Min, but there was always a wall in their way. He took down his opponents one by one until he was the last player standing and the battle was over.

Another Victory Royale for Tae Min.

Since it was the end of the day, Grey appeared in the battle warehouse along with the other one hundred players trapped in the game. He stood next to the others of his rank. Ben was right next to him. Kiri was still a few behind but had moved closer, and Tristan was just ahead of all of them.

Like he'd grown used to, the Admin appeared in front of them. "This concludes the third week of battles. Your rankings are posted on the board. Please keep in mind that you have five weeks left to be one of the top five ranked. This will be the only way to return to the real world. All remaining players will participate in the next season of battles."

Grey gulped. Five weeks? He tried not to

think about time passing, but five weeks didn't feel like enough.

Which meant he'd be stuck here for two more months.

When he already missed home so badly he could cry.

The Admin disappeared, leaving the players to themselves for the next three hours before mandatory "bedtime." Grey still wasn't sure that he slept during that time, but he did feel rested after, and that was always welcome.

"More practice?" Ben asked as everyone broke off into their squads. Things had settled since the beginning of the season when everyone seemed angry, as if people had accepted their fates. Though Hazel, a player that started with Grey, still trolled them frequently.

"I need a breather," Grey said. "You guys go ahead. I'll catch up."

Kiri frowned. "You okay?"

"Just need to clear my head before more Fortnite," he said.

"I bet the little baby boy misses home!" Hazel interrupted. She pointed a finger, and everyone stared. "Look at him! He looks like he's about to cry because he can't see his mommy."

Hazel's squad laughed.

Grey rushed away before his face made expressions he wanted to hide. He headed for his cabin and his bed. He wished he could fall asleep now, but that never worked. All he could do was lie there and think about everything he missed.

He wished his best friend Finn was there so they could talk about the game. Finn would know how to get better. He'd help Grey rank up. Finn would probably be like Hazel and be excited to be in the game, too, since he already loved to play it so much.

At this point, he even missed his little sister, Bella. She was always bothering him, but now he wondered what she was doing. How was she taking the idea of him being in a coma? He hated to think of how much his family was worried about him and wished he could tell them he was okay.

Grey squeezed his eyes shut. Crying wouldn't get him anywhere. Only a top five rank could do that, and he had to figure out a way to make that happen.

CHAPTER TWO

Grey heard the door of his cabin open, but no noisy footsteps followed. Not the familiar steps of Ben and Tristan, nor the louder ones of Lorenzo. He looked up to find Tae Min sitting on his own bed. Tae Min didn't look at Grey, but it still felt like he might speak. It had been three weeks, and Grey still hadn't heard Tae Min say a word.

"You do miss home," Tae Min said.

Grey gulped. Could he just talk to Tae Min? Ben had made it seem like the guy didn't like talking, but maybe it was different when Tae Min started the conversation. "Is it that obvious?"

"Is your home nice?" Tae Min asked.

"I like it." Grey didn't know how much to say.

Tae Min wasn't a gossiper, but Grey didn't want anyone to hear that he really was upset. Everyone already saw him as weak. "It wasn't perfect, and my family isn't rich or anything. But it's home, you know?"

Tae Min shrugged.

Did Tae Min not have a home to miss? No one had heard his real story, though there was plenty of speculation from other players. Grey decided not to pry. It already seemed like a big deal that Tae Min was saying anything to him.

"Keep building—not faster, but smarter," Tae Min said. "Don't wait for anyone to tell you. Just do it until you are better."

"O-Okay." Grey raised his eyebrows in surprise. Did Tae Min just . . . give him advice? Not that it was incredibly specific, but it still felt like a gift. "Thanks."

Tae Min nodded once, and then he lay on his bed with his back toward Grey. It was enough for Grey. To get any encouragement from the top player meant a lot, and he resolved to listen. Maybe the advice meant Tae Min thought Grey could get home if he just kept working on his ability to build.

Not faster, but smarter.

Grey wondered what that meant. There was still time before bed, so Grey jumped up and went back outside to find his squad mates.

The practice area was extra busy today, so perhaps the Admin's warning about only having five weeks left didn't impact just Grey. Some of the top squads—the ones in the top twenty ranks—sparred each other in giant structures that loomed high above where Grey walked on the ground.

The height of the buildings had scared Grey at first, but he'd gotten used to being up on precarious ledges. Kiri loved those kinds of builds—they only helped her snipe players better—so their squad accommodated.

Because though Kiri still might have had the lowest rank of them, she had the highest elimination count of all of them.

Grey worried she would leave them. Even now, he spotted her talking with the leader of a top twenty squad. Ben and Tristan stood several paces off, looking nervous. It wasn't the first or even the tenth time someone had tried to recruit her right in front of them.

"Please consider it," Zach, a skinny teen from Harlem, said with clasped hands. "You want to get home, right? Well, we can get you there much faster than your squad."

Kiri let out a long sigh.

Grey hung back to watch. Part of him didn't understand why she stuck around with him, Ben, and Tristan. She had gotten sucked into the game without having ever played because she'd lost a bet with her older brother. She missed her home just as much as Grey did, and he almost wanted her to go home more than he himself wanted to. At least he'd *wanted* to play Fortnite. Kiri never did.

"Look," she said as she put her hands on her hips. "Stop asking, okay? I'm not switching. Everyone had a go at me except for them. Who's to say you won't kick me out if I'm not spot on?"

"We won't!" Zach insisted. In all fairness, Zach seemed like a decent guy from what Grey could tell. He wasn't a trash talker, and his squad worked well as a team. "We're only looking for a person because Anya doesn't want to go home anymore. She and Veejay are a thing now, I guess."

Grey grimaced. He'd seen a few couples in the game, but he couldn't imagine deciding to stay just to be with someone.

"Sorry, I need to get back to practice." Kiri

walked away, leaving Zach to slump his shoulders and go back to his own squad.

Grey approached his squad, and Ben was the first one to notice. "Hey, dude. Get your rest?"

Grey nodded. "What have you been practicing?"

"Builds," Tristan said, though his eyes were on Kiri. "You could join Zach, you know. You deserve a better squad. You've gotten very good."

Kiri glared at him. "You want me to?"

Tristan shook his head. "No, but . . . we are holding you back. We can all admit that, I think."

Ben winced. "He's not wrong. We're lucky to have you still."

Kiri looked to Grey. "You think I should go, too?"

It seemed like Kiri would be mad if he agreed, but what else could he do? "It's not that I *want* you to go. It's just that . . . we'd all understand if *you* want to. I don't want to ruin your chances of getting back home this season. You've more than proven yourself."

Kiri was quiet for a moment. "Then you all just need to get better, because I'm not leaving the squad. Let's keep practicing, ay?"

"If you say so." Grey couldn't help but smile. Even though he felt guilty for holding Kiri back, he was grateful for a friend who wouldn't up and leave for their own benefit. He felt like he could trust her, and that made her an even better squad mate than her good aim. "Can we do some building? I want to work on build battles."

"We need that the most," Ben said as they all headed to the warehouse in the practice area. It was filled with an endless supply of weapons, items, and materials. "We'll never get past Hazel's squad if we can't build faster. Jamar and Sandhya are too good at that."

"I don't know what we are missing," Tristan said as they filled their inventory with wood, brick, and metal. "We build as fast as anyone."

"Well, we never have enough mats," Grey pointed out. He had never used up a full stack of materials in practice, but in game they were always short at the worst times. He thought of Tae Min. "And maybe it's not about being faster—but smarter?"

"That's a good way to think of it," Kiri said. "Maybe it's like reflexes? I mean, when I first started playing netball, I was rubbish and never scored. Then somewhere along the way I just learned when things felt *right*."

This sounded a lot like what Tae Min had

been saying. Grey just had to figure out what "building smarter" meant. He had an idea, which he wouldn't usually share, but he was getting desperate to rank up. "Maybe we could try solo building versus each other? Some teams rely on a couple good builders, but the top teams probably all know how to do it well."

"It's worth a try," Tristan said.

"I'll go up against Ben first," Grey offered. Ben was the best builder on their squad, and Grey needed to catch up to him at the very least.

Ben smiled. "You're on!"

CHAPTER THREE

Instead of building where everyone could watch, Grey and his squad moved farther out into the practice area. The place was the same as always, with the trees, buildings, and bushes not having moved. The sun had stayed in the same place in the sky, and even the clouds hadn't budged since Grey got sucked into the game.

But it hadn't always been the same, Grey had learned. There had been a handful of "patches" to the virtual reality version that they were stuck in, or times when the game had been altered. Ben and Tristan told him about them. The map in the battles had changed—Dusty Divot was once Dusty Depot and not a crater, and Tilted Towers was actually a pretty new location that hadn't existed when they first came into the game. Some of the weapons were removed, and others had their damage levels or speeds changed. Skins had been added and removed. For a day, there was even a jet pack that let players fly, but it was too overpowered.

Grey worried about facing a patch when he was finally getting used to the map and items as they were.

They picked a favorite hill on the outskirts of the ghost town where Grey first met Tristan and Ben. Hardly anyone came here to build, and they could talk and practice without the scrutiny of other players. Grey liked it that way. It was hard to learn when Hazel was constantly yelling, "You're doing it wrong!"

"So how should we do this, Grey?" Ben asked.

"Well, now that I've watched a lot of the top twenty . . ." Grey pulled at his shirt collar. Usually it was Ben and Tristan making the calls on practice—they did have more experience after all—but they had also peaked in the fifties in ranking so maybe they needed help, too. "It doesn't seem to always be about how high or fast but where the player puts the walls and ramps to get advantage. Like, all those weird angles. Tae

Min is always trapping people below him, not just building straight up."

"True," Ben admitted. "But how do we practice that?"

"I dunno," Grey replied.

"Maybe we try to shoot each other or block shots with our builds," Tristan suggested. "First to ten hits instead? No matter how big the build is?"

"I like that," Kiri said. "It will help me with my close combat. Still rubbish there."

Grey smiled, happy his idea was received well. "Ready then?"

"Let's do this! We only have a half hour left," Ben said.

Tristan and Kiri moved farther away so they would have their own room to build and fight. Ben backed away from Grey, a clever smile on his face as he pulled out the blueprint that indicated he was in building mode. Grey selected his wood materials, and he, too, now held a blueprint.

"On your mark!" Ben yelled. "Get set! Go!"

Grey immediately threw up a wall between him and Ben, only to find Ben had done the same thing. The walls began to build themselves plank by plank, and Grey's mind was already stressed about what to do next.

He used a ramp to connect to the wall that he'd made—he could shoot Ben from above if he got up there fast enough. But Ben had made a ramp, too, and he'd done it faster than Grey. A shot flew into Grey's shoulder, and his body blinked red to indicate he'd been hit even though in practice he didn't take damage.

"One!" Ben called.

Grey put another wall in the way, this time as a roof above the ramp he'd made. Ben's shots damaged it but didn't hit Grey. Moving around to the other side of Ben's wall, Grey put down two ramps to get a height advantage on his squad mate. He pulled out the AR he had and took a shot.

Ben blinked red.

"One back!" Grey smiled.

Ben used a wall to block Grey's view of him, and Grey had to switch back to build mode to put in more height. Now he'd created a floor above Ben, and as he went to the edge he was able to hit him two more times before Ben ran for cover.

Grey lost track of Ben for too much time after that. He couldn't tell if Ben had boxed himself in below or if he was building something else. As he peeked over the ledge, he got his answer in the form of a shot to the face.

"Two! Three!" Ben called.

Grey stood there for a second longer, taking another shot, because he was surprised to see what Ben had done—his squad mate had edited the roof to make a small opening to shoot from. It would be harder for Grey to get an angle on him.

It was a good move Grey hadn't thought about.

He needed to get more comfortable in editing walls after he made them. That was what slowed him down the most.

"Five!" Ben called after another successful shot.

Grey moved out of the way, trying to gather his thoughts for a move to counter this. Even though he had the high ground, he wasn't at an advantageous angle. Maybe if he built higher and destroyed that wall with the window . . .

He used a few ramps to get higher, but Ben shot at them and Grey came crashing down to the ground. If it weren't for practice mode, Grey would have been eliminated right there from fall damage.

Ben fired at Grey from another window he'd made, and in a quick five shots the match was over. Ben jumped out of the window with a smile. "I win!"

Grey nodded. "Yeah, you did. Those editing skills."

"I won, too," Tristan said as he and Kiri joined them.

"Shocking, I know," Kiri said.

"But that was fun!" Ben jumped around, hyped up on adrenaline. "I think that's a good way to practice! It's like what the top squads do against each other, but solo."

"Yes," Tristan said. "It will help us learn how to react to an enemy build. Let's do it again. I will fight Ben this time."

"Cool, me versus Kiri then," Grey said with a smile. They liked his idea, and he had a feeling this is what Tae Min could have meant. Building wasn't just about speed or good sniper angles. It was like a chess match to see who could outfox the other. And maybe if they could master that, they could make a bid for those top five spots.

CHAPTER FOUR

Grey and his squad had practiced as much as they could to prepare for the next day. While he didn't expect to be a million times better already, he did feel like he had more tools to use than just building fast. Building against Tristan, Kiri, and Ben helped Grey to improvise and think smarter, and he was sure that was the missing ingredient Tae Min had been hinting at.

As Grey entered the battle warehouse to begin the day's fights, he said, "Let's get some good build battles today."

"That means lots more mats," Tristan said.

"What about the shipping container yard then?" Ben said. "Those pallets give a lot of wood."

Tristan nodded. "It has a lot of loot, though more spread out."

"Sounds good," Kiri said.

"What was that? The shipping yard?" a familiar voice cut in. Grey turned to find Hazel and her squad. Even though they had proven they weren't a bottom squad, Hazel still made sure to troll his squad as much as possible. "Hey guys! Wanna go shipping yard?"

"Yeah!" Jamar said with a mean smile. "Good place for mats."

"Totally." Hazel folded her arms as she looked over them. "Let's outbuild these baby noobs and make sure they're homesick for another season."

"Just because we're young doesn't mean we can't beat you," Kiri said.

Hazel laughed. "A few lucky battles don't mean you'll beat us, kiddo."

"C'mon, Kiri," Grey said as he nudged her to keep walking. "It's not worth it. There's only one way to shut her up—proving her wrong."

"Good luck on that!" Hazel said as Grey's squad moved to the opposite side of the battle warehouse.

They sat in front of the rankings board, and Grey looked up at the list. If he would've ranked in the high forties after three weeks of playing in the real world, he would've been beyond proud of that. But in this virtual world, it didn't feel like enough. He stared at the names just above him—Hazel's squad, plus a few solo and duo players. There were so many above that, but right now those closer names were the ones they needed to climb over in the ranks.

They all leaned in to whisper. There were only a few minutes before the Admin showed up to start the day's battles.

"Guess we're not going to the shipping yard," Tristan said. "They will definitely be there."

"Let's just go anyway. We gotta learn how to beat them," Grey insisted.

"And how do we do that?" Ben's voice carried his frustration. "Me and Tristan have been stuck at this rank forever. I wanna beat them, too, but I got nothing."

"I don't know," Grey admitted. "But we can't just keep running away. How will we get better if we avoid really fighting?"

Kiri shook her head. "They'll just kill us, and our rank will drop."

"It doesn't matter if we're ranked in the nineties or in the fifties, does it?" Grey could hear the desperation in his voice as images of home filled his mind. "There are only five ranks that actually matter. How will we get closer to them if we're afraid of the people holding them?"

Grey's squad sat silent. Maybe he'd gone too far. When he thought about what he was saying, it did sound crazy. Desperate. But he didn't know what else to try and he really wanted to go home.

Finally, Tristan let out a long sigh. "He sort of has a point. If we keep telling ourselves we can't compete, they already have us beat mentally."

Kiri nodded. "My netball coach would say you gotta believe you can win. You can't give up before you even start."

"We've been playing scared," Grey said. "I mean, Hazel's super mean, but she never plays scared. Ever. She goes in believing she'll beat us and everyone."

Ben had stayed quiet through this, but he nodded as Grey spoke. "You're not wrong . . . The truth is I am scared. I wanna go back home, too, Grey. And maybe being reckless will teach us something, but it might set us back in ranks more than we could ever catch up. I don't know if I want to take that risk."

Grey could feel the fear as he looked at each person. No one wanted to lose rank—he didn't either—but he had a feeling that fear would hold them back more than anything else. He'd have to try a subtler approach. "Just one battle then. What about that? We go all out with no fear on the first one today, and then we can avoid Hazel and whoever else you want."

The squad looked at each other for a moment as they thought it over. Tristan spoke first, "I can agree to that if Ben can."

Ben pursed his lips. "Well, we always have at least one bad game anyway . . . May as well."

"Sweet as," Kiri said with a smile.

Battles will begin in thirty seconds!

Grey prepared himself. Even though they were already in the battle warehouse, they'd still be teleported to the ranking line that started and ended every day. In the blink of an eye, Grey stood in the line and the Admin appeared for her usual announcements.

"Welcome to Day Twenty-Two of battles!" the Admin said in her overly cheery tone. "To report on the state of the game—all items remain the same, and there are no changes to the map. No glitches have been reported, and no patches will be forthcoming for the time being. I wish you luck."

The Admin disappeared, and the countdown for the first battle began. Grey took a deep breath in an attempt to steady himself.

Grey and the rest of the players were transported to the Battle Bus, and he immediately checked its route. It would be flying over the northern part of the map, on a horizontal course from left to right. They'd go right over the shipping containers where they'd originally planned to land. Sometimes the route would be vertical or at a diagonal, and the path usually changed where people decided to loot.

"Still good on the shipping containers?" Grey asked.

"May as well," Ben said. He didn't sound very convinced. "Could be a fast game."

"Or a fast one for them," Grey replied. Positive thinking. He was determined to try it. Maybe he'd never brag like Hazel did, but there had to be a balance between confidence and humility.

"You should take the lead, Grey," Tristan said. "Since it's your plan."

"Okay." Grey had never taken the lead before. It made him nervous, but he reminded himself that his squad didn't expect much from this game anyway. "Three, two, one—and jump!"

Grey was the first of them out of the bus, and his heart raced as he flew toward the shipping containers. It was an unlabeled section of the map, between Tomato Town and Retail Row, and Grey worried he might miss it on the mini-map if he wasn't careful. They had visited the area several times in their battles but had never landed there first. Everything looked a little different from the sky.

Luckily, he spotted it with no trouble, thanks to the brightly colored containers that filled the area. The place was a maze with the containers acting as tall walls that created narrow paths.

It would be tricky to navigate. He wasn't about to pretend he knew where to land. "Tristan, can you help me out with loot locations? I don't know them."

"Start inside the containers," Tristan replied. "Go into an open one."

"Got it." Grey guided his glider into an opening in the nearest orange shipping container, and sure enough, there was a gold box in there. They opened it to find a sniper for Kiri and a blue-colored shotgun. "Ben, grab the shotgun."

"Aye, aye, captain," Ben said as he picked it up with its accompanying ammo.

Grey gave the shield to Kiri and the bandages to Tristan, and they moved on to the next open container as quickly as they could. He was surprised to find there was actually a lot of loot in the area. Though some of it was spread out, they broke down pallets for wood material on their way.

By the time they'd entered their fifth container and found a giant llama piñata, they were already sitting pretty with decent weapons and enough ammo, shield, and bandages to face a good fight.

"Okay, this place is so underrated," Ben said as they opened the llama. There were sticky grenades in there along with a few traps and more ammo. The best part was the 500 wood, brick, and metal that added to their stockpile of building materials. "So much loot!"

"But it took longer to get . . ." Kiri eyed the door. "And where's Hazel's squad? I haven't heard anything."

"Guess they lied," Grey said. "Or they assumed we'd chicken out if we knew they were coming here."

"Mayb—" The sound of pickaxes on metal echoed through their container, alerting them that they were not alone anymore. Kiri peeked out the door. "There they are. I saw Hazel's skin."

While many people liked to change up their skins—Grey was currently wearing the newest one he'd earned, a guy in a dino suit—Hazel always wore the same green-haired girl skin so everyone would know it was her.

"They must be coming from Tomato Town or Retail Row." Ben's voice was laced with fear. "They'll be stocked up."

"But we are, too," Grey pointed out. Luckily, his squad wasn't at the bottom of the yard but in one of the containers closer to the top. They had some height advantage. Grey gathered his courage. "Follow me, okay? No playing scared this battle."

Grey pulled out his building materials. He already had almost max wood thanks to the llama, so he built a ramp right out of the shipping container to get them to even higher ground. "Ben! Build walls behind if they shoot!"

"Got it!"

Grey kept laying down ramps and supporting walls until he got a good view of the shipping yard from above. He heard shots being fired, but he counted on Ben to take care of their protection from behind. Grey had to make sure the structure didn't collapse on them from all the fired shots.

Kiri took her own shots as they moved up the tower Grey built. "I got one low!"

"Focusing!" Tristan added his fire to Kiri's. "Downed!"

"They're boxing up," Kiri reported.

Boxing up meant their team was trying to heal the downed player in the protection of walls. Grey stopped building and pulled out his AR. "Everyone, focus on them!"

Their shots brought down the protective walls, and someone on the enemy squad kept trying to rebuild. Another enemy shot their way, and Grey almost lost all of his shield. He moved back to build mode to put up their own wall, but he didn't want to let them revive the downed player.

"We're pushing," he said.

"Are you crazy?" Ben asked.

"For this game, yes." Grey built a ramp and then more floors so they could get closer to Hazel's squad. "Who's got sticky grenades?"

"Me. Throwing." Ben, despite his fear, threw the grenade now that they were in range. It blew open the protective box, and now that all the walls were down, they had a wide-open shot on Hazel's squad. And the high ground to boot.

Grey switched to his weapon and opened fire with the rest of his squad.

Kiri eliminated Sandhya.

That must have been the downed player. The other three were on the move, but one fell just as Hazel threw up a wall to protect them yet again.

"Get that downed!" Grey called out.

Ben tossed another grenade and it stuck to the wall. Once they blew it open, Grey's screen read: *Ben eliminated Jamar.*

But Hazel and her remaining squad mate, Guang, had disappeared behind a few walls. Grey wanted to chase them, but then Tristan said, "Grey, storm's coming."

Grey glanced at the map—the next safe zone was past Tomato Town, and they were even farther outside that. They only had thirty seconds . . . and that wasn't enough. At least, it wasn't until Grey spotted something among Sandhya's loot. "Get that launch pad and let's get out. We'll have to get Hazel and Guang later."

"They'll be behind us trying to get into the eye, too," Kiri said as they grabbed the launch pad.

They left the shipping yard behind, and Grey kept glancing back, waiting to see Hazel and Guang. The storm was closing in fast, and he imagined Hazel and Guang might already be taking damage from it. If his squad used the launch pad, anyone else who saw it would be able to use it, too. Grey had a feeling Hazel would be out for revenge after what happened in the shipping yard. She'd still be confident she could eliminate all of them even with only half a squad.

Maybe confidence wasn't always a good thing.

But Grey could count on Hazel's confidence, and he could use it to his advantage. Once they got to a higher hill, he said, "Use the launch pad now."

"Hazel and Guang will see it," Ben said.

"But we'll land first," Grey said. "We can get them."

"Putting it down," Tristan said as the storm consumed them.

Grey began to take one tick of damage a second, since it was only the first storm. He jumped onto the launch pad and flew into the air. The option to open his glider came up, and he did so. He and his squad soared faster toward the eye of the storm, where they would be safe from the purple haze's damage.

He hoped there'd be no one waiting for them on the safe side, because he wanted to focus on the enemies behind them. "See anyone else?"

"Not so far," Ben replied as they glided into the eye of the storm. The damage stopped, but Grey had already lost a third of his health.

"Hazel and Guang are airborne!" Kiri announced as she let a few shots fly. They made a loud, echoing noise that anyone in the area would hear. "Ugh, missed."

"Don't waste your ammo," Grey said. They would need that for future fights, and he had an idea of how they could eliminate these two players in a worse way. His avatar pulled out the blueprint and pencil to indicate Grey was in build mode.

"You wouldn't . . ." Tristan said. "That's so mean."

"I'm sending a message." Grey began to use the extra metal he got from the llama to build a wall right on the edge of the storm. He made it two stories high and then added a ramp and flooring so he could get up higher and make it even taller. He could see Hazel and Guang turning to the right in attempts to avoid his barricade, but other than that they were helpless, floating in the air. "Build more on the right! They're turning."

"Got it!" Tristan said.

Grey moved that direction as well, adding walls on top of Tristan's. Maybe it was a waste of materials, but it was satisfying to see Hazel and Guang smack into the barricade while still taking damage on the other side of the storm.

They shot frantically to break down the wall, and Grey got another idea. "Anyone have a bouncer?"

"I do!" Kiri said.

"Place it right there." Grey couldn't help but laugh as Kiri put it down, because Hazel and Guang went flying back into the storm as they bounced off it. Grey's entire squad burst into laughter as the notifications popped up in their vision:

Hazel was lost in the storm.

Guang was lost in the storm.

"That was the best thing I've ever seen," Ben said through his laughing. "But we gotta move."

"Yeah," Grey said. They were on the edge of Tomato Town, and the next storm moved closer to Loot Lake. It would be a challenge to get that far. "We'll have to skip Tomato Town. Half of it is already in the storm anyway."

"Let's pick up stuff on the way to Loot Lake," Tristan said as they started moving that direction. "We'll need a lot of mats for building there."

"Probably," Grey said.

While there didn't seem to be anyone else coming from their direction, they would soon be facing whoever had started in Pleasant Park, Tilted Towers, and even Dusty Divot and Anarchy Acres—those were all popular places to land among the top squads. There were just under forty people left on the map, and they were sure to be well-equipped after surviving those areas.

The terrain between their location and Loot Lake was mostly fields and trees, so they broke down what they could for wood. There was a small building with some extra ammo and shields, and they were lucky to find a gold chest among a patch of trees.

"Yes!" Kiri grabbed the glowing orange weapon, knowing they'd give any legendary sniper to her anyway. "Bolt-Action, my favorite!"

"Can I take the shotgun?" Tristan asked. "Then I can double pump."

"Sure," Grey said. He was happy to have their best shots better equipped for the upcoming fight. "How are you guys on mats?"

"Not maxed out yet," Ben said. "Loot Lake is gonna be all about builds—it's so wide open."

"Okay, let's stock up then." Grey broke down the trees around them, making sure to keep an eye out in case anyone heard the noise. The battle may not have been over yet, but they had beaten Hazel's squad, and that was always a victory in Grey's book. If they could just *keep* doing that, he'd take it.

Every other kill this game was gravy.

CHAPTER FIVE

Grey did not like Loot Lake. While there seemed to be okay items, it certainly didn't live up to its name. It also felt like a vulnerable position with the sprawling lake making it wide open for spotting other players. While they hid on the ground among the trees, he could already see several towers being built on the opposite side of the lake.

"We're late to the party," Grey said. The adrenaline from the last fight had worn off, and so had some of his courage. "Not gonna lie, I don't know what to do."

"Be aggressive," Ben said. "That's what you said we're doing this game."

"It hasn't gone too badly, honestly," Kiri said. "Down to twenty-three players."

Grey took a deep breath. He'd already spent all his bravery on Hazel's squad. "All right, time to build up. Maybe Kiri can get some snipes."

"Sweet as. Let's do it."

"I'll use my mats," Tristan offered. "Save yours for the push, Grey."

"Good idea." Grey was glad to have Tristan offering ideas because he was beginning to feel out of place as a leader now that they were facing the top twenty players. He tried to shake it off. This had been a good game for them. He should be happy.

Tristan built their tower quickly, which was a good thing because they began to take fire the moment they had more than three stories. The players across the lake had obviously spotted them by now, and Grey's squad needed to put on the pressure before their enemies destroyed their building.

It would have been a good time to have a rocket launcher, but none of them had had the luck to get one.

"Build out over the lake a little!" Kiri said. "I can't get a good—"

Kiri's gear spilled from her while Grey barely processed the two swift shots that came their way, and when he read the notification he knew why:

Tae Min eliminated Kiri by head shot.

"Ugh!" Kiri sounded madder than usual. "I swear he's out to get me!"

"You *did* head shot him once," Ben offered. "Tae Min never gets—"

Tae Min eliminated Ben by head shot.

"Oh, come on!" Grey said. He still hadn't seen where Tae Min was, but he clearly had a good sniper nest for himself. And a powerful weapon. "Take cover!"

Tristan opened a hole in their floor—and just in time, because another shot hit their walls as Grey and Tristan boxed themselves in their tower for protection. This was going about as well as Grey had pictured it would. He tried not to be mad, but after Tae Min gave Grey advice . . . Grey thought Tae Min might be on their side for some reason.

Apparently not.

Grey heard the sound of a rocket launcher, and he knew things wouldn't end well if they stayed in the same place. "We'll have to go on foot. Around the lake."

"May as well," Tristan said.

There was no way they'd get anything built at this point. Everyone on the other side of the lake had their number; plus they had Tae Min on their tails. Grey and Tristan left their tower, and Grey searched desperately for where Tae Min might be.

A loud sniper shot sounded, and Grey realized it was coming from the center of the lake where there was a house perched on a small island.

Tae Min eliminated Mayumi.

Tae Min eliminated Zach.

So that was where he was. Tae Min must have gotten to the lake before anyone else and snagged that prime spot for himself. It wasn't always a good position, but under the current circumstances, it was perfect. He'd be able to pick off anyone around the lake while all the other squads fought it out at closer range.

Grey and Tristan soon came upon a wonky tower, where there was obviously a build battle happening high above them between two other squads. The tower was a mess of ramps and walls, but the base was small and weak.

"Shoot it down." It was all Grey could think to do. They'd never be able to build up to the players at this point, but maybe they could bring them down here or destroy the tower entirely.

"Watch for traps," Tristan said as they took down the lower walls.

Grey did, but there was nothing. Finally, he took out the last remaining support on the ground, and the upper walls began to break apart. He shot above them at the players, who had finally noticed their tower was going down.

No one fell like Grey had hoped. Instead, they dropped a launch pad and jumped. Soon it was a deadly free-for-all as they descended on Grey and Tristan.

Grey shot wildly at all the players in the air, and he got two before he was downed.

You were eliminated by Hans.

Tristan followed soon after. Grey looked at his ranking of eighteen and didn't know how to feel. He knew it was good—probably the best he'd get of the day—but he felt like he could have done better, too.

Tae Min ended up winning the battle, as usual. Grey watched as he eliminated player after player who tried to approach the island. Some were able to get close, a couple even made it to land, but Tae Min got them in the end.

As Grey appeared back in the lobby, he started moving right to the practice area. He could feel his squad following him, but no one spoke. He couldn't figure out why he was so mad, but he just wanted to keep practicing and he didn't want to talk to Hazel or whoever else felt like trolling them today.

"What's up, Grey?" Ben said as they entered the practice warehouse. "We did really good! But you seem mad about it."

"I don't know," Grey said. But he did know. He couldn't look at them. "I froze. We got to the lake, and I just blanked."

He felt like he had let them down.

"You were brilliant!" Kiri said in surprise. "Yeah, you froze, but you were flash up to that point!"

Grey shook his head. He hadn't felt very "flash." "I mean, we got Hazel's group . . . but other than that, I was kind of a fail."

"We finished in the top twenty-five," Ben said. "That's not a fail. That'll probably be our best game of the day . . . unless you're up to try again on leading. I think you might be a natural leader—it's just you've been so quiet until now that none of us knew it."

"Me?" Grey shook his head. "I'm not good at that."

Grey was never the leader of anything. He was always the one people didn't want to listen to. Or the one who didn't speak up. He hated having that responsibility. It always left him feeling like he did right now—like he hadn't lived up to expectations. He regretted pushing everyone to be more aggressive. If he knew it meant he'd be suggested as the leader, he wouldn't have done it.

"But I think you're good at it," Ben insisted. "Just like Kiri didn't know she could snipe, but you saw it. Maybe you don't see your own abilities."

Grey felt like a weight had been put on his chest. As he looked to Tristan and Kiri, he hoped for them to disagree. "You guys don't think that, too, do you?"

Kiri shrugged. "Sorry, mate, I agree with Ben."

"I think we should at least try the whole day with you leading," Tristan said. "You only froze because we don't reach that late in the game often. But if we keep getting there because of you, we will all learn."

Grey let out a long sigh. "But what if that last game was just luck? I could tank us in the next ones . . ."

"It could have been luck," Ben said. "But, Grey, you thought of stuff on a different level when you let go and let yourself play confidently. Like, it was so awesome. Seriously. You didn't even see how you were building and responding to Hazel's group. I was shocked. We need you to keep doing that."

"Sorry. I need to think about it," Grey said.

"Sure," Tristan said. "Go think."

Grey walked out of the practice warehouse, his mind racing from the battle and from what his squad was asking him to do. It was easy to pretend to be confident for one game. But to be the leader every time? It seemed crazy that Ben and Tristan would want him to do that when they had so much more experience. He couldn't possibly be better than them at leading when he had only been playing for a few weeks.

Grey entered the dense woods near the practice area. On the first day he was stuck here, he remembered how Kiri had run into this place when she was upset. It wasn't quite like a real forest, more like a cartoon version, but there was something that felt more private about it. No one came here since it wasn't in the practice area or very near the cabins where they slept.

Finding a spot under a tree, Grey sat and tried to wrap his mind around taking on the leadership role. It scared him. And he wasn't sure he could make it past that fear.

CHAPTER SIX

Grey was supposed to be thinking about leading a squad and if he really was good at it, but his mind went right back to missing his real life instead. He had been so excited to go to seventh grade, and now he might not even make it out to go. His mom had taken him to test into advanced math, and she had been so proud when he succeeded.

He missed her hugs. Her smile. Even the way she'd call his name when she needed help.

Squeezing his eyes shut, Grey refused to cry. It wouldn't help anything and would only make him feel even more homesick.

All he wanted to do was go home. Even thinking of playing more games today made him want to cry. He didn't want to play anymore. Not today or tomorrow or ever. If he managed to make it out of the game, he'd never play again. This wasn't how leaders thought—leaders were like Hazel, endlessly confident and determined to win.

Finn would have been a good leader, and he would have been happy to do it. If only he was here with Grey, they'd probably be top twenty already.

But Grey wasn't like Finn. Grey always thought of himself as a sidekick, and he didn't mind it. It was easy for Grey to suggest his squad be more aggressive, but it was another thing to be the one taking charge to do it.

He'd just have to tell them he couldn't.

"Grey?" Kiri's voice came from behind and startled him.

He wiped at his eyes, realizing a few tears had escaped despite his best efforts. "Yeah?"

Kiri appeared from behind the trees, stopping in place when she spotted him. If she saw the tears, she didn't point them out. All she did was sit next to him. A moment of silence passed before she said, "You're homesick, ay?"

Grey cringed.

"Me too," Kiri said. "It's bad. I've never been

away from home this long. Never away from my family at all."

Grey gulped. Even though she was admitting her own homesickness, he still didn't want to talk about his. "Yeah?"

Kiri nodded. "I miss my mum the most, but everything else, too. School was going well for once, and at this rate I'll miss out on netball try-outs. I miss real world things, too—food, nature, animals. Even just noise."

Maybe Grey wasn't the only one struggling so much. "Did you have any pets?"

"A cat," Kiri said. "An orange stray we named Carrot. He would follow me home from school, and we ended up keeping him. You?"

Grey shook his head. "But I've always wanted a dog. My mom's allergic, though."

"That's no good," Kiri said.

There was another long gap in conversation after that. Grey had no desire to fill it. He didn't understand why Kiri was there if she wasn't going to say anything more. He thought she would try to convince him to lead. He didn't know if he wanted her to do that or not, or if she even could.

"Can you guess what I miss most about my mum?" Kiri said after several minutes of quiet.

"No," Grey said.

"I miss her cheering me on." Kiri let out a long sigh as she stretched out her legs. "She came to all my games, and she thought I was some superstar. She'd tell me someday I'd be in the Olympics. Even when I lost, we'd get Indian takeaway after and she'd tell me I'd win the next one. Mum made me feel like I could do it . . . I wish I could hear her say that now."

Grey felt a lump grow in his throat and the sting of tears prick at his eyes. It sounded a lot like something his own mom would do.

"If our mums could watch us battle," Kiri kept going, "do you think they would say we're rubbish, or would they cheer us on? Would they want us to give up against Hazel or try our best?"

So this was Kiri's plan. She was smart.

Grey could picture exactly what his mom would say about all of this. She would tell him to fight. She would say he could do it even if he didn't think he could. Grey could picture his mother's smile if he told her he was the leader of a squad. She would say he'd be good at it.

Grey leaned his head on the tree trunk, looking up through the fake leaves. "You guys really want me to lead, huh?"

"Yeah," Kiri said. "Can I ask you a question?"

"Sure."

"While you've been here, how many times have you had an idea but didn't say anything?" Kiri turned so she was facing him, and her dark eyes pierced his resolve.

Grey shrugged. Because he couldn't put a number to it.

"I have a feeling it's a lot. Hundreds, maybe." Kiri punched Grey lightly on the shoulder. "Today you didn't keep those ideas to yourself, and look what happened! Sometimes it's not about how long you've been playing, ay? You have ideas Tristan and Ben haven't come up with in all the time they've been here. Don't be afraid. What if that is what gets us home?"

"What if it's what keeps us here?" Grey blurted out. "It'd be my fault! And you'd all hate me."

Kiri raised her eyebrows. "Is that what you think?"

"It's too much pressure," he replied. "And I already crumbled under it after one game."

"You're too hard on yourself! It was the first time you led, and you did so well. You're bound to get better." Kiri shoved him. "What about just today, then? You convinced us to try one game being more aggressive. How about just today leading? Like you said—only the top five spots really matter. We can't be afraid to try new tactics."

Grey sighed. "Using my own words against me."

"They were good words." Kiri smiled at him, and something about it made him feel more at ease. "The words of a leader. They gave us the courage to do something different."

Grey almost explained that he was just being desperate and homesick, but he was still too embarrassed. Even when Kiri had been honest with him. Most of all, he could picture his mom telling him to give it a try. She wouldn't want him to give up. She would believe in him. Maybe if he kept thinking of that instead of missing home, he would have the motivation he needed.

"Today," Grey said. "I'll do it today and see what happens."

"Sweet as, mate!" Kiri jumped up. "I'll go tell the others. You clear your head and such."

"Okay." Grey watched her go, a small smile on his face. Kiri was a good squad mate. He was glad to have her encouragement even though he was still nervous to lead. He tried to focus on it only being one day. He could lead for one day.

One minute until the next battle begins! the now-familiar announcer's voice said.

Grey closed his eyes and gathered every ounce of courage he could find in himself. He pictured his family cheering for him as if they could watch from wherever they were at the moment. Though the idea still made him homesick, it also pushed him. Maybe this way he could use it as motivation instead of letting it hold him back.

CHAPTER SEVEN

Grey couldn't help but be nervous for their second game of the day. When he was only leading for one game—a game everyone was sure would be a throwaway—it wasn't so bad. But now they thought he'd be good.

He was pretty sure they would all die first because of him.

It's only for a day. Grey would have to take it one battle at a time.

"Where should we go?" Ben asked.

Grey realized they expected him to decide. And he had no idea. So, he went with the first thing that came to mind. "How about we go back to Loot Lake? May as well try to figure it out when it's so close to all those top-player areas."

"Good thinking," Tristan said. "I can guide us through the house on the island."

"That'd be great." Grey was surprised in particular by how supportive Tristan was being. He hadn't even wanted Grey to be in the squad, and now he was happy to help teach Grey the ropes of leading.

Grey didn't know what that meant, but he'd take it.

As the Battle Bus opened, Grey took one last deep breath to steel himself before the fights ahead. "Jumping in three, two, one!"

Grey flew through the air. He was happy with his choice of Loot Lake because it was an easy place to spot as the biggest body of water besides the oceans. Impossible to miss. The closer they got, the easier it was to see the house in the middle of the lake, and Grey used his glider to aim for that roof.

"We've got friends!" Ben announced as they broke open the roof.

Sure enough, when Grey looked up, he spotted a full squad with their gliders right behind them. It didn't look like Hazel, but he couldn't count on it because she and her squad mates could have changed their skins.

"Find the weapons first!" Grey immediately

replied. There would be weapons lying around that weren't in chests. Sometimes they weren't the strongest, but he had learned over the last weeks that having a weapon of any kind made the difference in the beginning.

"This way!" Tristan said.

"We need to spread out," Grey said. "Ben, take Kiri with you the other way. Get gear."

"Got it." Ben and Kiri broke off and moved downstairs while Tristan and Grey cleared the attic. There was a hunting rifle lying out, and Grey let Tristan take it. Grey was able to pick up a minigun and ammo, and they found a chest with a shotgun, a shield, and bandages.

Just in time, too, because shots had been fired and Tristan had taken damage. Grey turned— some of the squad had built up to the roof and were right behind them. Grey opened fire with the minigun, jumping around to make it harder for his opponents to aim. The minigun spat ammo out at a rapid pace, inaccurately, but in close quarters it mowed down their enemies.

Tristan added in a few shots, and soon the downed players gave up their gear.

You eliminated Petra.

Tristan eliminated Eric.

"Nice," Grey said, his mind racing with adrenaline. Shots still sounded in the area, though he couldn't see enemies. "Ben, Kiri, you guys okay?"

"We need help," Ben said.

"They're on us," Kiri said. "Taking damage."

"This way, Grey." Tristan directed Grey downstairs to where their squad mates had blocked themselves off from the remaining attackers.

Grey dropped his bandages for Ben and Kiri to use, since he hadn't taken much damage. He'd used all his minigun ammo on the fight upstairs, but he still had the shotgun. "What did you guys pick up?"

"A few impulse grenades and a pair of basic ARs," Kiri said. "One of them has to have a purple or orange weapon—I only took one hit but it nearly got me."

"Okay, follow me," Grey said as he used a small shield. He used the edit tool to open a door in the wall that was taking fire. He raised his shotgun and tried to aim for the opponent, but she ducked behind the far wall. Grey rushed her position, determined to take her down.

Both players were in the next room, and he opened fire. He heard the sound of a trap being laid. "Don't run in! Trapping."

Shots came from behind him, and soon the players were eliminated. They spilled their gear, but Grey had to be careful to destroy the trap first before going in. Like Kiri had guessed, one of them had a purple weapon. Grey let Ben take it.

With that squad gone, Grey's was free to ransack the rest of the house and island. Now that he was in the same area as Tae Min had been last game, it didn't seem as ideal as he once thought. It was right out in the open, too, and if he hadn't frozen, he thought there might have been a way to take out someone who was positioned here. Grey just wasn't prepared. He needed more experience so he'd know what to do in every situation.

He'd have to get that experience through practice.

The eye of the storm was closing in soon. While Loot Lake was still well inside, it was clear the next storm would likely put them in a worse position. They needed to make their way west, toward Pleasant Park.

Grey built a ramp down to the water, which was really a giant puddle you could walk through. It was unnerving to be out in the open on the lake, but they seemed to be on their own after taking out the squad. It wasn't until they got to the shore that Grey spotted a solo player, and Ben took him out with a few shots.

Ben eliminated Robert.

"Poor guy," Ben said. "Still hasn't made much progress, has he?"

"Yeah . . ." Kiri said. Robert was another player who started when Grey and Kiri did. He was an older man, and so far, no one had taken him into their squad. He was one of the lowest-ranked players with an average rank in the eighties.

The closer they got to Pleasant Park, the more people they found. And this time Grey regretted not having stocked up better on materials. They had gotten some wood, brick, and metal on their way but not nearly enough. He was starting to see why Ben always said they could use more. Grey had been spoiled by the llama in the last game and didn't realize what an impact it had made.

"Back off, box up," Grey said as they took heavy damage from another squad. He closed them inside a wooden structure for protection, but it wouldn't last long. "We need to regroup."

"They won't let us go so easily," Tristan said.

"Pretty sure that's Hans's group. He likes that skeleton skin."

Hans's group was the one Tristan had left for. He was quickly kicked out the next day when he didn't keep their rank up to par. They were still a good squad even with only three players, always in the top thirties or higher.

"Well, we'll have to—" The sound of a rocket launcher stopped Grey from speaking, and he winced because surely that would come their way.

But to his surprise, their box still stood.

"Another squad on Hans!" Kiri announced.

"Let's move then!" Grey opened a door through the back of their barely standing box and moved north away from the fight. It might have seemed cowardly, but it wasn't always the right move to dive in if you knew you didn't have the tools. They needed more loot. More ammo. More materials.

Then they could stand a fighting chance.

As Grey led his squad away from the crossfire, the sounds of the fight waned. He assumed this meant no one was following them, and it was a relief. They still had time before the next storm shrunk the map, but at least they were going the right direction and didn't have to worry about getting stuck.

They broke down trees as they ran and were lucky enough to happen upon a chest that had a couple med kits to replenish their health.

There were still fifty-one players on the map, but Grey was sure that would dwindle based solely on the eye's next location. Not many people landed in Junk Junction or Haunted Hills, so most people would be rushing toward the northwest corner of the map. Grey hoped, unlike last battle, that they would be one of the first squads to get there and not one of the final groups.

Hans eliminated Guang.

Hazel eliminated Mayumi.

Hans eliminated Hazel.

Grey always felt better when he out-ranked Hazel. It had become a benchmark for his own squad's performance. Now he could rest easier, thinking the two games he'd been leader were two games they'd beaten Hazel.

"Soccer stadium might still have loot," Tristan offered as they made it to the outskirts of a big structure. "It was popular when it first appeared in place of the castle but now not so much."

"May as well." Grey hadn't been there too

many times, but they did need more loot, and it was on the way.

"There's usually a chest in the semi," Tristan said.

They swung around the building to where several semi-trucks were parked on one side. Sure enough, the back of one was open and there was a golden chest. The guns inside weren't much better than what they had, but there was a bounce pad and a few sticky grenades. They restocked on ammo, shields, and bandages as they foraged around inside the stadium's halls. But the place was missing one thing Grey really wanted—more wood for building.

There was metal and brick to break down, but it was obvious they wouldn't be getting more wood if they stayed here. The area was also quite open, which reminded him of Loot Lake. That big soccer field felt like a danger zone, though with materials you might be able to defend yourself.

Grey wanted to move on, but as the next storm began, he checked his map to see if the one after might be at Junk Junction or Haunted Hills.

It was right over the stadium where they were.

"I guess we're setting up shop here," Ben said.

"Yup," Grey said as he broke down more metal. It took the longest to build, but it was what they had, and he wanted to save the wood in his inventory for when they needed to build faster. Besides, a stronger metal at the bottom of their tower probably wouldn't hurt if they had the time to build it.

The sound of explosions and gunfire sounded closer, and Grey began building right where they stood in the stands of the soccer field. His squad followed him up the tower, and at their taller viewpoint Grey could see the source of the commotion.

A build battle was happening just south of the stadium.

Grey couldn't tell who was fighting, but the ramps and walls appeared at lightning speed. From the off-kilter appearance, he could tell the players were using the build to block off their opponents in attempts to get the higher ground.

Normally, he would watch and wait for one side to win, but today he knew he had to stop hanging back and take the lead.

"We're going in," Grey said as he began to build floors out over the soccer field to take them to the build battle in the sky. Maybe this time instead of freezing up, he could get the jump on this battle.

CHAPTER EIGHT

"**A**re you crazy?" Ben yelled as they all followed Grey onto the sky bridge he had built. They were at least five stories high already and not even close to the height of the build battle in front of him.

Grey started throwing down ramps to gain altitude. "Maybe?"

"Stop freaking out and shoot!" Tristan said. "We're in range and they are focused on each other."

"Fine!" Ben said as he pulled out his shotgun.

The players jumped around on their sky tower, and Grey was almost glad he was the one building because he was sure he'd miss every shot. But his squad mates took shots when they could, and their opponents definitely knew this battle was a three-way deal now.

Fire returned on them, and Grey had to throw up a few walls to protect them. He frantically connected their bridge to the structure of the other squads—that way they had something to jump onto if the floors got shot out from under them.

"Where are those sticky grenades?" Grey asked.

"Here!" Kiri said as she threw one as far as she could to the walls above them.

When it exploded, it blasted a hole that exposed the players above. Tristan took several shots, and one of the players fell to a crawling position.

"Throw more!" Grey insisted.

Kiri used all the sticky grenades she had, and soon there were openings everywhere. When they didn't get immediately patched up, Grey realized something vital: The enemies were out of mats.

Which meant he and his squad had the upper hand if he could build well enough. He had just over four hundred wood left, and he began to build higher. While Grey's squad didn't have the high ground, their awkward positioning right below the enemy made it hard for them to take shots when there were still players up there to deal with.

Lorenzo eliminated Diana.

Gear spilled above them, so Grey knew that was local elimination. He saw an impulse grenade explode, and a player went flying off the mountainous tower.

Lorenzo didn't stick the landing.

That "fall damage" elimination notification always seemed particularly embarrassing, but Grey also thought it was funny. There seemed to be two or three players left above them, so Grey built around to find a good angle on them.

Kiri eliminated Veejay by head shot.

"How do you do that?" Ben said. "Every time!"

"Not *every* time," Kiri replied.

"Pushing up!" Grey announced as he began to use ramps. With two players left, it felt like the right time to gain the high ground. Surely the remaining enemies didn't have full health after a drawn-out fight.

The storm was beginning to close in again, and they needed a breather before the next fights if they wanted to survive. Grey switched to a weapon the second he had built their ramp higher than their opponents, and he let off a shot as the one wearing a triceratops skin tried to hide.

You eliminated Anya.

"The other one is climbing down for cover," Tristan announced.

Grey reacted instinctively by jumping down a couple levels to find the player. He didn't want to lose this elimination. To his surprise, the person placed a bounce pad on a nearby wall and flung himself at it. The guy went flying off the tower, and for a moment Grey thought the guy was out to eliminate himself. But then Grey remembered that bounce pads made it so you didn't take falling damage, and he realized it was an attempt to make a getaway.

So Grey used the bounce pad, too.

His squad mates yelled at him, though he was too focused to pay attention to the words. He shot off the tower like a rocket, and for a moment he panicked that this was a bad idea. But then he positioned himself so he could aim at the guy who'd landed on the soccer field. He let off a couple shots while he flew, missing one but hitting his opponent on the second.

The glowing items poured out as the avatar fell to the ground.

You eliminated Julio.

"Gone mad, haven't you?" Kiri's voice sounded in Grey's ears even though they weren't close.

"You guys wanted me to lead," Grey said as he looked over Julio's items. There weren't any materials like Grey had guessed, but there were several more bounce pads, a grenade launcher with no ammo, and a few small shields he hadn't had time to use. Grey picked up everything—he liked that bounce pad trick. He'd never thought to use them like that before, but now his mind raced through all the new possibilities.

"We're coming to you," Ben said as they all used the same bounce pad to get down from the tower safely.

As they came down, Grey took a look at the map to see how the storm would shrink next. He realized, as leader, he was already thinking more about this aspect of the battle. He hadn't noticed how much less he paid attention when Ben was leading and how important it was to stay aware of positioning.

"The circle is closer to Junk Junction next,"

Grey said. "Let's keep moving. I have no mats after that."

"I'm low, too," Tristan said.

"I got nothing," Ben added.

"Take mine." Kiri offered all her wood. It was only a couple hundred, but it was better than nothing. Grey picked it up and they headed for the next zone. They were once again in the top thirty, and he felt good about that.

A whopping ten people got lost in the storm as it closed in on Junk Junction, showing just how difficult a position it was to get in. Grey imagined there were some people on the opposite side of the map who had spent the entire battle just trying to stay inside the safe zone. They had had battles like that, and they sucked.

There were only two people in Junk Junction, and with a full squad, Grey's squad was able to eliminate them without much trouble. After that they stocked up on items and destroyed everything they could for materials while Kiri kept an eye out for anyone coming into the area. She had found a port-a-fort and stayed perched up there while the rest of them gathered below.

The storm began to shrink, and Grey's materials were almost maxed out when Kiri called from her sniper nest. "We have big incoming! They're fighting each other!"

"You stay up there," Grey said. "We'll go in and see who we can pick off at closer range."

"Sounds brilliant!" she said as she opened fire.

Grey followed the direction of her shots, and sure enough, the builds were going up at the edge of the newest safe zone. "Tristan, ramp us up there."

"On it." Tristan began to drop his ramps, adding a few walls in for support in case anyone tried to blow up their build from below. Grey had found some ammo for his grenade launcher, and he used it liberally to disrupt the fighting and building in front of them.

The sound of a rocket launcher hit Grey's ears, and he said, "Need a launch pad!"

"Dropping one now!" Ben answered.

Ben placed it on the floor Tristan just laid, and Grey jumped onto it. He sprang into the air and deployed his glider. He took a couple hits, but they only ate his shield. There were several players building and fighting, and the chaos was a lot to take in.

Grey wasn't sure they'd survive, but he wanted to take down as many as he could. He pulled out the minigun now that he had plenty of ammo for it, and he unloaded on anyone and anything in sight. Walls and people went down, and Kiri cleaned up any player who fell to their knees.

But Grey had already lost his shield, and now he took damage though he tried to box himself in. Tristan and Ben weren't faring much better.

"This might be it, guys," Grey said as he attempted to use a bandage. It was interrupted by someone breaking the wall and shooting him.

He was officially downed.

"We went out in a blaze of glory!" Ben said as he, too, ended up in downed state.

"We took five more with us though," Tristan offered.

Grey's vision went to black and white, and his gear scattered around him. He had finished at rank fifteen for the battle, which was a few better than last time. Kiri made it to rank ten in her sniper perch before Tae Min once again took her out. It was as if he wanted to make sure everyone knew there was still at least one person better at sniping than Kiri.

The battle ended not long after that, and when Grey appeared back in the forest by himself he smiled.

Rank eighteen the first game.

Rank fifteen the second.

Maybe he wasn't so bad at leading. He didn't expect it to go that well every time—people would soon catch on and take them more seriously—but it felt good to start the day out in the top twenty.

CHAPTER NINE

By the time the day was over and Grey stood in the ranking line, he almost couldn't believe how many spots he'd jumped. He'd gotten several new skins, including some really cool full-body ones for making it to the top twenty-five. The Admin appeared and went on with her normal speech, but Grey only looked at the ranking board behind her.

He'd gone up five ranks. That was a lot for one day.

Everyone in his squad had done at least as well. Tristan out-ranked Hazel, and the rest of the squad was mixed with hers. If they had even a couple more days like today, they'd be higher than Hazel's squad, guaranteed.

Grey had been so distracted with their standings that he didn't notice the Admin disappear. It wasn't until he saw the angry face and green hair that he snapped out of it.

Hazel grabbed him by the shirt collar. "How'd you do that, noob?"

"Do what?" Grey asked. Maybe he had found some confidence on the battlefield, but face-to-face with Hazel was a different matter.

"You know what!" Hazel shook him. He wasn't afraid she'd hurt him, since pain didn't seem to be part of this virtual reality, but he could never find the right words when someone was being so aggressive. "Your ranks! Did you find an exploit? You *had* to have cheated!"

Grey's eyes went wide. "We didn't cheat!"

"Don't lie." Hazel pushed him back. Her glare was enough to scare anyone into telling the truth. "Tell us all, or I'll report you."

"We did not cheat!" Kiri jumped in front of Grey, much braver than usual in the face of Hazel. "We just switched up our roles."

"Yeah, right." Hazel put her hands on her hips. "You can't improve that much in *one day* just from a role swap."

Grey let out a sigh. He should have known

even doing well wasn't enough. Instead of respect, they only got accusations of cheating. Everyone in the warehouse was looking at him. This was just what he'd feared—people would take notice of their rank jump, and the next day his team would not get so lucky. Maybe it was a good start, but tomorrow and every day after would be the real test.

"Kiri, let's go practice," Grey said.

"But—" Kiri looked back at him like she couldn't believe he didn't want to defend himself.

He shook his head. He didn't want anyone even knowing for sure that he was the one who'd taken the lead. Their suspicions were enough. They could all see his kill count had gone up. Some might have even watched Grey's squad after being eliminated in game. "Practice."

"Fine," she said as she glared at Hazel.

"I'm going to report you!" Hazel said. "You totally cheated!"

Now it was Ben who stepped in. "Go ahead. The Admin will review everything and show you got beaten by us all day fair and square. We have nothing to hide."

Hazel folded her arms. "We'll see about that."

Grey gave up and kept walking. He didn't

like all the attention. He also didn't like being called a cheater, but he knew what Ben said was true. They hadn't cheated. And if Hazel really did report them, it would be a waste of her time.

The idea of getting reported still made him nervous. Maybe he hadn't cheated, but Tae Min's advice had been a major catalyst in his improvement today. More than Grey could have ever imagined it would be. His encouragement changed how Grey saw himself and gave him some motivation to try new tactics.

And then there was Kiri's pep talk. She'd helped him get over his homesickness and use it as motivation and not a detriment. He wouldn't have led nearly as well as he had today without both of them.

That wasn't cheating, was it? The Admin had to have records of that as well as everything in the battles.

It couldn't be considered wrong. The Admin had said before that sharing and practicing was allowed within the appointed times. He'd just gotten help to improve like most people here had done in some way or another. Hazel was just being a sore loser, and he shouldn't expect anything else from her.

"Don't worry about her," Ben said as he caught up to Grey's pace. "People report, but the Admin is fair and there's rarely been a case of actual cheating."

"Someone really has cheated?" Kiri said in surprise. "How do you even do that in virtual reality? I guess I can see hacks on a computer or something."

"They found a bug," Tristan said, "and exploited it instead of reporting it to the Admin. It was in the first season we got stuck here. The guy was in the top five, but his rank was stripped two weeks before the end of the season and he had no way to get back up in time without his cheating. He got home in season three, though."

"That's mental," Kiri said.

"Yeah," Ben said. "All the other times, the reports were just salty players who couldn't accept when people got better."

"I have more ideas for practice." Grey was determined to stay focused. After leading for five games, he had seen where some of the gaps in their play could be fixed. "Kiri, we need to teach you how to block incoming fire with walls and ramps. Sometimes we just can't protect you. You rely on us too much."

"O-Okay," Kiri said, though she seemed surprised by the topic change.

"It'll make you even better," Grey said as they entered the practice warehouse. He grabbed an endless supply of bounce pads. "And the rest of us need to practice with these."

Tristan gave him a skeptical look. "Why these? They're so situational."

"I don't think so," Grey insisted. "We haven't been using them to their full potential. I also think they could help us practice aiming."

"I don't see what you mean," Ben said as he picked out a variety of weapons. "But given how we did today, I'm not gonna argue."

"Lots of those top guys are shooting midair, while they're on the move or when they're bouncing on these," Grey said. "I missed a ton of shots because I haven't really thought of doing that. Aiming while build battling or while on these bounce pads—we're gonna need to get better at that if we want to keep competing. Everyone, get some so we can use them against each other."

"Okay," Tristan said. "But if we're stuck here next season, don't wait for three weeks to offer up all these good ideas."

A pang of guilt hit Grey. "Sorry. I wasn't sure if any of my ideas were good."

"Well, now you . . ." Ben trailed off, his eyes on something behind them.

Grey turned, and to his surprise, he saw Hans and his squad. They were looking right at Grey's team, so they weren't necessarily here to stock up for practice. It felt like they were looking for Grey. He gulped back his nerves. "Can I help you, Hans?"

"You played well today," Hans said. He was a short, older guy who Grey thought might be in his mid-twenties. He was from Norway, and he led his squad, but that was about all Grey knew about him. "If you continue to do so, I would like to extend an invitation to practice against us."

"Oh," was all Grey could say.

He must have looked as surprised as he felt, because Hans smiled. "It is not a joke. Not everyone is like Hazel. I appreciate good competition. You are still new, but your building creativity shows promise."

"Th-Thanks," Grey said. "We'd love to practice if you think we're up to the challenge."

"If you stick at your rank for a couple more days," Hans said. "We'll talk, yah?"

"Definitely." Grey didn't know what else to say as Hans and his squad picked out weapons, so instead he motioned for his squad mates to follow him outside.

As they walked to their usual practice spot, Ben said, "Did that really just happen?"

"I think so," Kiri said.

"It's a big compliment," Tristan said. "Hans is very picky about who they practice with. As you know, he'll even kick someone out of squad if they're not up to par. He'd rather have only three elite players than deal with one weaker one."

Tristan was referring to himself.

"You're not weak," Ben said, though he'd been the one abandoned when Tristan had left their squad a few weeks ago.

"I am compared to them," Tristan said. "I can admit that now. I thought I was better than I am, but I see now there is room to improve. We'd learn a lot practicing with them. I learned a lot just in one day."

"It would be a massive help," Kiri said.

"No pressure," Grey replied. There were already so many reasons Grey wanted to reach the top ranks, but this only added one more. His shoulders felt heavy with all the responsibility now on them. The only thing that would relieve the weight was practice, and that was exactly what he intended to do.

CHAPTER TEN

Resting did not feel as rejuvenating as it usually did. Grey and his squad had spent every minute they could practicing their aim while moving. Grey worked with Kiri so that she could get comfortable throwing up her own walls to block incoming fire. She hated switching between building and weapons, but she got better at it with the practice. Maybe it wouldn't save her from Tae Min, but every little bit helped.

The day went . . . okay.

If Grey hadn't had a day where he finished in the top twenty every game, he would have been proud. But it was spotty at best. As he worried, people took their squad more seriously now. Instead of enemies focusing on their build battles when Grey charged one in progress, both teams turned on Grey's instead.

Grey's squad rank was in the thirties. They traded either just beating out Hazel's squad or just losing to them. Their ranking didn't move up at all for the day but instead went down a hair.

Grey went to bed that night frustrated, even though everyone else said they were doing well.

As they all gathered in the battle warehouse before the day's fights, Grey said, "Change up your skins again. Every battle if you want."

Ben nodded. "That seemed to help."

After the first two games of getting targeted yesterday, Grey tried that. It wasn't perfect, but it seemed to help get Hazel off their scent.

That didn't mean she hadn't reported them like she promised.

The more Grey thought about it, the more insulted he felt. Instead of being seen for his hard work, everyone whispered about the possibility of him cheating. He'd never do that. Even if the opportunity was there.

As the Admin popped up to begin the day, Grey's nerves hit an all-time high. Tristan and Ben had prepared him for how the ruling would go, but it still felt like there was a chance he'd get in trouble.

They *had* improved at an abnormal pace. What if he'd been cheating and didn't know it? Anything seemed possible in a place like this.

"Welcome to Day Twenty-Three of battles!" the Admin began in her cheery tone. The smile was always the same, no matter the news that came out of her mouth. "All items remain the same, as do all the locations on the map. There was one report of cheating, made by Hazel against Grey, Ben, Kiri, and Tristan. The game footage has been reviewed in its entirety, and the judges have ruled no cheating has taken place."

"What?" Hazel yelled. "That's impossible! They were crap a few days ago!"

The Admin turned to her. "While their improvement is remarkable, it is not due to any exploits or bugs within the game. Footage does reveal that their squad practices in nearly every spare moment, with a calculated 30 percent more practice than the average squad. This was the only major difference we could determine. Perhaps it will be a lesson to other squads, which is why I share this information now."

"That much?" Ben whispered. "I didn't realize . . ."

"Ugh," Hazel huffed. "How boring. Thanks, Mom."

"I am not your mother," the Admin said. "I wish you all luck in your battles."

The Admin disappeared, and everyone was transported to the Battle Bus before they could say anything else about the matter. But Grey did feel better knowing he was in the right no matter what Hazel claimed. He took a look at the map to see the route the bus was taking—it was in the south, moving across only the bottom of the map.

"I bet the storms will push us north," Tristan said.

"Or it'll be a fight fest all in the south," Ben said.

"Let's go Lucky Landing," Grey said. It was far in the south, but he liked the location. It was styled like some of the buildings he'd seen when his family visited Japantown on their trip to San Francisco. The thought made him homesick, but he told himself to fight hard if he wanted to get back. "Jumping in three, two, one!"

Grey leapt from the Battle Bus and scanned

the sky to take inventory of where other players were gliding. A lot still headed for Tilted Towers, while others were on their way to the Salty Springs and Fatal Fields areas. More north. A better position if the storm circles popped up that direction.

But Grey stuck with Lucky Landing. A handful of other players also looked to be joining them, and his heart raced because their moving-target practice would be put to the test right away.

"Ben and Tristan, you pair up and grab weapons," Grey said. "Me and Kiri will do the same. We don't have time to gather as a group."

"Good thinking," Ben said.

"I'll follow you," Kiri said.

Grey landed on the balcony of one of the tan buildings. There was a basic shotgun on the ground with ammo. "Kiri, take it."

She did, and they ran inside, though he saw other players going in through the roof. If he could get the loot first . . .

Shots fired, and he took damage. Grey ducked behind a wall, cursing because the room they were in had nothing to use. Kiri stood beside him, trying to take shots when she peeked out from behind the wall. But she took a hit, too, and neither of them had shields or bandages.

Grey broke down some of the furniture for mats and threw up a wall to protect them. But it wouldn't last long. "Run back outside! Get to Tristan and Ben!"

Kiri began her run, and they both jumped off the balcony and toward the dots that indicated where Ben and Tristan were. But the enemies were still on them, and gunfire rang in Grey's ears.

He knew this wouldn't end well.

But he ran right behind Kiri so if they got hit he'd be the one to take the damage. Sure enough, he went down. Kiri stopped, but he yelled, "Keep going! I'm done for!"

She did as she was told, much to his relief. They didn't have any resources to do much else. No materials to build protective walls. No weapons to fight back with. Grey knew this happened. But as his vision went black and white, he felt like it wasn't fair at all.

Lorenzo eliminated you.

Grey was dead at rank ninety-five for the game. It was his worst performance for days. While he was already feeling pretty salty about it—he'd beaten Lorenzo's crew several times— he tried to be the leader he needed to be. "Don't worry about me, guys. Do what you can to get the highest rank possible for the game."

"Sorry, Grey," Kiri said. "I ran out of ammo."

"It happens." Grey switched over to Kiri's feed so he could still watch where his squad was. "I'll spectate you and try to help you guys if I can."

"We have gear at least," Tristan said.

"And now we know it's Lorenzo's squad. We can deal with them," Ben said. Grey was happy to hear him speak with more confidence. Ben had been playing scared for a long time without realizing it was holding him back.

Grey's squad did take out Lorenzo's. It was close and all of them took significant damage, but they ultimately got out of Lucky Landing alive.

The battle didn't last much longer for them after that, though, since they had guessed wrong on the storm location. The next safe zone was farther north, the border halfway through Fatal Fields. They barely made it inside in time, but there were people waiting for them. With low health as it was, they were all eliminated.

They finished ranking in the seventies.

"Sorry, guys," Grey couldn't help but say as they all waited for the rest of the battle to play out. He decided to switch to Hans's feed to watch him, since maybe they wouldn't be earning practice sessions with Hans's squad after all.

"Don't beat yourself up, man," Ben said. "It happens. One bad game doesn't erase all the good ones we've had recently."

But it felt like it did. And Grey wished it didn't have to be the first one of the day when they had to teleport back to the battle warehouse where everyone else would be. Of all the hard parts of being stuck in Battle Royale, he might have hated that the most. In the normal game, you walked away from a battle and moved on. None of the enemies could talk to each other. In this hacked virtual reality, people could rub your losses in your face.

"Let's just win one today," Kiri said. "That'll cancel it out."

"Okay, sure . . ." Grey let out a short laugh. They had only gotten one Victory Royale, and a lot of it had been luck. They were in the perfect position. They had gotten a llama. They had the best weapons.

"It could happen!" Kiri insisted. "We've gotten close a lot of times in the last couple days!"

Grey sighed. She wasn't wrong, but it was

hard to picture winning right after a battle where he ranked ninety-five.

The game ended with Hans's squad taking a rare victory from Tae Min, and they all appeared in the battle warehouse. Sure enough, Lorenzo was already pointing and laughing at Grey. "See, Hazel? Grey's not cheating! Maybe you just suck!"

"Shut up!" Hazel yelled back. "You eliminated him before he even had a weapon, right?"

Lorenzo didn't say anything to that.

"That doesn't even count!" Hazel shook her head. "Brag about taking him down when they at least have something to fight back with."

Grey raised an eyebrow. Was Hazel . . . defending him? It didn't feel quite like that, but her words were the nicest that had ever come out of her mouth when it came to Grey. It still didn't make him want to stay there. "Let's go practice, guys."

Ben, Tristan, and Kiri looked at each other instead of moving.

"What?" Grey said.

Kiri pursed her lips as she looked around the room. "Maybe we should talk outside. It's a squad thing."

"Okay . . ." For the first time in a few days, Grey wasn't the one leading his squad outside to practice. It was Kiri in front. And instead of going to the practice area, she moved into the forest by the cabins. They all sat under a tree. And it was quiet for so long Grey began to feel like he was in trouble.

"Can someone tell me what's going on?" Grey demanded.

"You're stressed as, mate," Kiri said. "We just think you might need a second to chill instead of practicing."

Grey glared at her. "You heard the Admin—we practice more than anyone else. How do you think we got here?"

"There's such a thing as too much practice, too," Tristan said. "When I was preparing for a rock-climbing competition, I would want to practice until I couldn't move. But my coach always made me stop because he didn't want my strength spent before a competition. You're pushing too hard, Grey."

"Yeah, man," Ben said. "We're not saying we want to stop practicing, but let's hang out before the next battle, okay? Let's think of something else besides Fortnite."

"Like what?" Even to Grey, his voice sounded stressed, which deflated his desire to defend himself against their claims. He let out a sigh, realizing he felt tense all over. But he didn't know how to relax. "So much is riding on today, guys. We can't lose sight of our goals."

"Talking about something else doesn't mean we don't want to win," Kiri said.

"Yeah," Ben said. "I was leading before you, right? I know what you're dealing with. I got so in my head . . . It wasn't until you took over that I realized how much pressure I was putting on myself. And it didn't make me play better. I played worse. I had us all playing scared because of my stress—you can't deny that, can you?"

Grey didn't answer, though he did agree.

"We're a team," Kiri said. "You don't have to carry everything on your own. We all want to get home. No one expects *you* to take us there—we all have a responsibility to pull our weight."

"Yeah," Tristan said. "So stop putting all that weight on yourself. It's not helping any of us."

Grey got a little choked up, so he couldn't speak right away. He had been putting the fate of everyone on himself, and it was nice to hear that they didn't think it was all on him. He was still stressed out, but it felt like he could breathe a bit easier. "Thanks, guys."

"Thank you," Kiri said, "for working so hard to make us better."

Ben nodded. "We've all gotten better because of you."

"You might be a noob to this game," Tristan said. "But you are good at finding ways to improve skills quickly. Your game knowledge will only improve."

Ben punched Grey's shoulder. "Then you might be unstoppable."

Grey smiled. It was hard to think of himself as some unstoppable player. "I thought we were supposed to be talking about non-Fortnite stuff."

"Right!" Kiri said. "Shall I teach you about netball?"

"Sure," Grey replied.

And so they talked, and even laughed. For a very small moment, Grey was able to forget about the battles. It was a small gift, and he was glad for the break when all was said and done.

CHAPTER ELEVEN

The break proved to be just what Grey needed to get back on track. Their second game went much better, and they beat Hazel's squad by five ranks. The third game, they finished just behind them. In the fourth game, Hazel's team took a low rank loss like Grey's had in the first game.

So it all came down to the last battle of the day.

The pressure still threatened to consume Grey, but he tried to take a deep breath as they appeared in their Battle Bus seats. Maybe they wouldn't do well. Maybe Hazel's squad would still out-rank theirs. Maybe Hans wouldn't want to practice with them. Grey told himself it would be fine. If they could make this much progress without Hans, then they could keep improving regardless. And then out-ranking Hazel's squad would naturally follow.

It would be better if it happened today, but it could happen tomorrow or the next day.

Because Grey wouldn't stop fighting to get home.

"Let's go to the soccer stadium and rotate to Pleasant Park," Grey said as he looked over the map. Maybe he didn't have quite enough courage to face Tilted Towers yet, but he felt like they had figured out how to skirmish at least enough to get closer. And they needed more practice with multi-squad fights anyway. "Spread out and grab the loot you can find, then we'll meet up."

"You sure?" Kiri's voice was laced with nerves. She hated being on her own.

"You can do it," Grey said. "Call for backup if you get in trouble."

"Okay." Kiri took a deep breath.

"Chances are there won't be many people there," Tristan offered. "It will gear us up before Pleasant."

That was the plan at least. The Battle Bus opened, and Grey took the jump with his squad.

It was a jump he'd grown to enjoy, a quiet before the storm of the fight. The island looked so nice and peaceful from above, with its bright green terrain and cartoon-style buildings.

Grey deployed his glider, taking care to notice that a few more people besides his squad were headed in their direction. A handful were also going to Anarchy Acres, which was on the east side of the soccer stadium. While it made him nervous, he told himself they could handle it.

He just needed to get a weapon first.

From the air, he spotted a gun lying out in the stands. He aimed himself so that he'd land right on it even though there was another player trying to do the same thing. He was just slightly ahead, but not far enough that he felt like it was a sure thing. "Grabbing the shotgun. Don't worry about me. Get. Weapons."

"Aye, aye, captain," Ben said. "I see an SMG. I'll back you up."

"Going under the stands," Tristan said. "One went that way."

"Taking the chest in the semi," Kiri said.

Grey swooped down on the shotgun and ammo, turning immediately to face his opponent. He took a pickaxe to the face, but he equipped the weapon and let off a few shots. The female avatar fell to the ground crawling. "They're a duo at least."

You eliminated Selena.

"Ah!" Kiri's scream in the comms meant only one thing—someone had found her.

"Jump and shoot!" Grey said. "We are coming!"

Grey ran through the stands, meeting up with Ben on the way. There were a few items lying in the aisles, and he picked them up as he went. The best was a pack of C4, which could take out half a house if needed. Grey almost never got it in battles. He'd save it for when they really needed it.

"No! Sorry!" Kiri's health bar on the left side of Grey's vision went red, meaning she'd been knocked down. He wished he could run faster, but the game made all their speeds the same in a battle.

He was starting to regret telling them to split up when a notification popped up: *Tristan eliminated Francois.*

"I got you," Tristan said in the comms. When Grey made it to the outside of the stadium, he spotted a metal box where Tristan was protecting Kiri while he revived her.

"Did he go right down?" Grey asked.

"Yeah," Tristan said.

"Must have been a duo then," Grey said with relief. "Think there's one more solo."

"Anyone pick up bandages or med kits?" Kiri asked.

"I got a med kit," Ben said as he dropped it for Kiri to use. "That was close."

"Too close," Kiri said.

Grey tried to push off the guilt. He had to remember that his squad didn't expect him to keep them alive all the time. They had to learn how to survive as well on their own as they could in a group. Kiri was still weak at that, but she would improve with practice in and outside of the battles. "Let's keep moving."

They cleared the rest of the stadium with ease, running into the last player in the area who had taken a lot of the loot while they fought. They divided the goods, each of them leaving with a few weapons and shields and bandages. Plus Grey got more C4 and Kiri picked up a grenade launcher. Tristan walked away with traps and Ben took the launch pad.

The first storm was due to come in one minute, but they were well within the radius of the safe zone, so Grey didn't worry about it too much. He was more concerned by their lack of materials. If they needed to build battle, they were currently at a severe disadvantage.

"Get wood," Grey said as he used his pickaxe to break down trees. It always felt like it took too much time, but he had yet to regret having extra materials on hand.

When they reached the outskirts of Pleasant Park, it was clear there were players there. Not only from the sounds of gunfire and explosions but from the builds and looted houses. The place didn't look much like a nice suburban neighborhood anymore but instead like a battle zone.

"Two in the nearest house," Tristan said.

"Using C4." Grey threw one at the wall and detonated it. While it wouldn't damage any of his squad mates, it would hurt him if he was in the fire. So, he stayed back and waited with his gun to see what it would reveal.

The house's walls exploded, opening a huge cavity. Someone went down in the blast, while another was crawling on the second floor. Kiri eliminated them first, and they all ran inside to get the loot and materials their opponents had dropped.

Even though the storm had shrunk the map just once, there were only thirty people left. Grey assumed there must have been a big fight somewhere, or maybe several somewheres. Usually there were still more people to face. They had only picked up five of those eliminations, and Grey itched to find some more now that he had materials for build battles.

"Hazel's here!" Ben yelled as he shot out the window. He took damage in return. "Those green pigtails give me nightmares!"

"Roof!" Grey built a floor and walls outside another window. He had faced Hazel's squad enough at this point to know they wouldn't just walk through the house when they got there. They would build ramps up to the second story or even to the top to get the jump on them.

So Grey would build higher, and hopefully faster.

Because they were beating Hazel this game. They had the resources, and he was determined to make sure she knew it had nothing to do with cheating. Grey had worked hard, and he wanted to prove that paid off more than bragging, trolling, and reporting people who didn't deserve it.

Shots fired all over, and it was hard to avoid

damage, but Grey put up as many walls as he could to block the incoming hits.

His squad got their own hits on their enemies, but it wasn't enough to down any of them. As the siren sounded for the next storm, Grey realized this would get sticky soon. Pleasant Park wasn't in the safe zone.

He thought about using the rest of his C4, but he felt like it wasn't quite the right time.

A rocket launcher sounded, and it wasn't from Hazel's squad. Grey spotted another group across from the open soccer field. They were building over to them. Grey didn't want to lose the eliminations to another squad, but he decided he needed to act on instinct.

"Retreat!" Grey called. "Dropping one C4!"

He threw it behind him as they moved toward the storm's border, detonating it to deter anyone who might follow. The build they'd made crumbled, but it wasn't tall enough that any of his enemies took fatal damage. Everything about the fight would go wrong if they stayed. He could feel it.

It wasn't easy to get out, since players fired on them, but his squad used walls to protect their retreat.

The storm would close in on Loot Lake, and Grey wanted to take the northern path to the lake instead of trying to fight their way through the army at Pleasant Park. But it would put them in the storm for a moment.

"Everyone have bandages?" Grey asked. "'Cause we'll be in the storm for a bit."

Everyone replied that they did, and he was also surprised no one argued with him. Grey hated being in the storm, though it was sometimes inevitable. At least this path would put them in a decent position going into Loot Lake, and he hoped they'd have time to recover.

Hans eliminated Jamar.

So it was Hans's squad at Pleasant Park. Grey was glad they had left. It looked like Hazel had stayed to fight them. At least that meant no one was following them into the storm.

Grey waited to see more eliminations of Hazel's squad, but none came. Instead, there were different notifications:

Tae Min eliminated Hans by head shot.

Tae Min eliminated Mayumi.

Tae Min eliminated Farrah.

Nothing came after that for a bit, so Grey figured the rest of Hazel's team had made a run for it with Tae Min in Pleasant Park. He must not have had the resources to run after them, but Grey expected that to change by the time they all made it to Loot Lake.

"Four from Anarchy," Ben said as they approached the lake. Anarchy Acres was just north of there, so it wasn't a surprise when so many had landed there this battle.

Shots came in, and Grey was pleased when Kiri threw up some shielding walls to protect them. Grey built a few ramps to get a higher position and then switched to his shotgun. He got a hit down before the other squad replied with their own protective walls.

"Grenade launching!" Kiri announced. The sound wasn't nearly as loud as a rocket launcher, but it was still enough to make the other team panic. The walls exploded, and at least one player was downed.

"Keep up the pressure!" Grey said as he shot at the fragile wooden walls they kept trying to use for protection.

"Bounce pad?" Ben asked.

"Sure!"

Once Ben set it down, they all bounced on it and flew closer to the enemy team. Grey let off shots in the air, having gotten used to doing it in practice. They were able to down the whole of Lorenzo's team, and it felt good to have one more behind them before going into the next phase.

Because there were only twelve people left.

That meant it was Grey's full squad, Hazel's remaining three members, Tae Min, and another four people he wasn't sure about.

Grey couldn't count on another Victory Royale against Tae Min, but he still wanted to beat Hazel.

The house on the north side of Loot Lake appeared to have already been looted, so Grey kept his eyes out for those four remaining mystery players. He wasn't sure if they were in a squad or not—he couldn't recall if the other usual top players had already been eliminated.

But something told him there was a player in the house.

"Tris, can you check the house on your own? I feel like we have a hider," Grey said. "I want to set up on the camp island."

"Sure." Tristan moved into the house.

The smaller campsite island, just north of the big house island, wasn't far from the lake shore. Grey, Ben, and Kiri jumped as they walked

through the lake, keeping their eyes out for enemies. "Kiri, keep a lookout while we build."

"Yeah, mate," Kiri said.

Tristan eliminated Robert.

"On my way to you," Tristan said.

"That poor man," Ben said. "He must have
been hidden this whole time. I guess that can get
you a good rank if you're lucky."

"Boring way to do it, though," Grey said.

Grey and Ben began to build up, while Kiri
stayed by them and peered out her scope occa-
sionally. Grey stopped at five levels, wanting to
save the rest of their materials in case they needed
to push out onto the lake. It had only been a few
days since the last time he faced this scenario, but
he already felt better equipped to not choke like
he did before.

Besides, this time he had two C4 left. If there
was ever a good time to use it, this next fight
would be it.

"Tower going up on the west side," Kiri
announced as Tristan met up with them. Kiri was
looking through her scope. "It's Hazel's squad."

Grey was already forming a plan. It was risky,
but they had the resources to make it happen.
"Ben, you're on bridge building. We're going to

bait them into a fall if we can—gotta put our C4 and grenades to use."

"Gotcha." Ben began to build out into the lake area. He used ramps to protect them and offer extra height.

Tae Min eliminated Rosita.

Tae Min eliminated Junnichi.

That was two more of the mystery players. Grey had no idea where they went down, but he had to guess it was on the Pleasant Park side of the map, based on Tae Min's last location. So maybe his squad was a bit safer where they were.

Hazel eliminated Hui Yin.

And that was the last mystery player. Grey could tell Hazel's squad had turned their attention to him now, as they began to take more fire and the enemy building moved their direction. Instead of using the sniper, Kiri had the grenade launcher out and was lobbing several in the direction of Hazel's squad in attempts to break their bridge.

Just when things looked like they were going down, Grey saw the launch pad drop. Hazel, Sandhya, and Guang flew up into the air and deployed their gliders.

Grey instinctively took over the building,

constructing walls and a roof in hopes that Hazel would land on it.

"What're you doing?" Kiri had switched to her sniper, but Grey's build blocked her shot. "I had that!"

"Run back!" Grey put down his C4 and ran for his life.

He waited until Hazel, Guang, and Sandhya landed, and then he detonated the C4. The explosion rocked them all and blew up anything that Hazel could hope to stand on. They fell, and Grey knew it was too high to survive. He couldn't help but laugh as all their gear spilled out in the lake below.

"Tae Min gliding!" Tristan yelled out as he fired at one more person in the sky.

Kiri joined in, and Tae Min joined Hazel's group in the lake.

Victory Royale!

"Now it's really Loot Lake," Grey said.

Ben let out a laugh. "Good one."

As the game ended, the victory began to sink in for Grey. They had done it. They beat Hazel for the day. They'd even gotten a Victory Royale. If that wasn't a sign of good things to come, he didn't know what was.

CHAPTER TWELVE

As Grey appeared back in the battle warehouse after a long day of fights, he couldn't help but smile. It felt good to end a day on a victory. It felt even better to look at the rankings while the Admin said her usual speech—he and all of his friends outranked Hazel and her squad now.

"That was flash as, mate," Kiri said once the Admin disappeared for the night.

"So flash," Ben repeated. "If I ever get out of here, I'm bringing 'flash' to Utah."

Kiri laughed. "Good!"

"That's it!" A loud voice cut off all the other conversations. "I can't take it anymore!"

Grey would have expected it to be Hazel, but instead it was Sandhya, her squad mate.